The Secret of the Bamboo Trail

AuthorHouse™
1663 Liberty Drive
Bloomington, IN 47403
www.authorhouse.com
Phone: 1 (800) 839-8640

ILLUSTRATIONS BY:
DESIREE RESETAR

Published by AuthorHouse 03/28/2015

ISBN: 978-1-5049-0380-6 (sc)
ISBN: 978-1-5049-0417-9 (e)

Print information available on the last page.

authorHOUSE®

The Secret
of the
Bamboo
Trail

Written By

NANCY CALIGURI

DEDICATION

To Jase & Kira – May you always see the beauty.

Lotus Blossom lives in the Village of the Rising Sun with her friend, Leaping Tiger and her dog Foo Foo.

One day Lotus Blossom was curious about beauty. She asked
Leaping Tiger, who she called Ty, if he knew where to find beauty.

Lotus Blossom wonders, what is beauty?

Ty said, "we will have to go to the House of Scrolls
and ask the Old Scholar about beauty."

Lotus Blossom said, "but to go to the House of Scrolls,
we will have to enter the Bamboo Trail."

The next day they started out on their adventure
to find out the secret of the Bamboo Trail.

On their way to the Bamboo Trail, they pass the women of the village. Lotus Blossom asked if they knew where to find beauty.

Lotus Blossom and Ty were getting closer to the Bamboo Trail.

Just ahead was the entrance of the Bamboo Trail. Lotus Blossom asked Ty if he was brave enough to enter. He said, 'yes' and off they went into the Bamboo Trail.

They ask the animals of the Bamboo Trail if
they knew where to find beauty.

Lotus Blossom and Ty were so excited to make it through the Bamboo Trail into a field of flowers and dragonflies.

Just ahead is the House of Scrolls!

As Lotus Blossom, Ty & Foo Foo enter the House of Scrolls looking for beauty, they realize the secret of the Bamboo Trail.

The Old Scholar was happy that Lotus Blossom & Ty had discovered the secret of the Bamboo Trail on their journey.

The secret is that beauty is everywhere!

The End

CPSIA information can be obtained at www.ICGtesting.com
Printed in the USA
BVOW10s2029060415

394982BV00004B/4/P